MOONLIGHT
TRAIL
MIYO HUNTER

MOONLIGHT TRAIL

MIYO HUNTER

CONTENT WARNING

This book contains:
    Graphic depictions of violence.
    Mature sexual situations.
    Nonconsensual kissing and groping (not between main characters).

If you object to violent imagery, cursing and spicy scenes, this is not the series for you.

-xoxo Miyo

For Roxie

CHAPTER 1

JENNY

Everyone knew that the wishing well delivered one's heart's desire—at a price. Perhaps it wouldn't give exactly what was asked. But it certainly made it easier for that heart's desire to come about. Many considered it a bit foolish, perhaps even desperate to resort to the wishing well. But I was running out of time.

The wishing well was a pool of water in the heart of the old growth forest that almost seemed to absorb the light of the moon.

I threw in my offering—a perfectly round stone dabbled with a single drop of my blood to show my sincerity. The slight ripples from the center of the pool were silvery. They seemed almost weighted by magic, thick and iridescent with the moon's blessing.

I shut my eyes, concentrating.

Please.

My fists clenched at my side, shaking with the force of my desire.

Please make me a wolf.

Shifting didn't happen for me, on the full moon when I

came of age. It didn't happen on the full moons for the following three years. Each year, I had stood with the other hopefuls who'd come of age, directly under the full brightness of the moon.

In recent years, the pack had grown. I watched as most of my peers received the blessing of the moon, shifting into their wolf forms. Then as the younger cohorts shifted, discovering their wolf form. Then there was me. Still fully human.

Waiting uselessly.

Father had sat me down after dinner last night. His words echoed around my head even now.

Perhaps it would be better if you didn't attend the next coming-of-age ceremony. If the moon goddess was going to choose you, it would have happened already. It's becoming an embarrassment.

I grit my teeth, as I brutally forced his words out of my mind.

It wasn't true. I still had a chance. It was rare, but there was such as a thing as wolves who bloomed later in life.

My twenty-second birthday was coming up. There was no record of anyone shifting after their twenty-second birthday.

I had one full moon left to make it happen; it was only two weeks away.

Only two weeks left.

I knew that I had a wolf within. I don't know why the moon goddess chose to make me wait, but I knew that it was a part of my destiny. It was a truth that resounded through me, a truth that I could feel in every inch of my being. Everyone doubted me, even my own family. But I would prove them all wrong.

I was already pretending not to see the disappointed

look in my parent's eyes when they thought I wasn't paying attention. When I passed my former teachers and coaches. Their expressions told me that they had hoped for more from me. I was a walking mass of wasted potential. They'd written me off already.

Until the last ripple smoothed into stillness across the wishing well, I pleaded with the goddess.

Thank you for hearing my wish.

I rushed down the path that everyone called the wishing trail. I'd prefer to stay out of sight. It wouldn't be long before my absence was noted. It wasn't forbidden to visit the well, but it would result in an awkward question that I'd much prefer not to answer.

I was on the part of the trail made of cobblestone, which was hard on my shoes. The heels ended in delicate points that were stately and elegant walking across marble hallways and awful for navigating this rocky terrain. I'd left immediately after dinner. It would have taken too long to hike all the way up to my quarters to change, so I'd just gone out with my inappropriate footwear.

It would all be worth it, as soon as I stepped out in the glow of the full moon and—

I walked straight into something that felt like a brick wall. I fell backwards, arms flailing, falling flat on my butt.

I looked straight at the brick wall and the wall looked back at me—a wall of muscle. Attached to a muscular man. A man who was currently staring down at me in slack jawed surprise.

He pulled himself together after a moment and held out his meaty hand. I reached for him, letting him help me up, and felt a spark burst across my palm. The burn was intense, searing deep within me, rooting me to the spot.

I immediately knew what it meant. Everyone who

looked at my skin for the rest of my life would know exactly what it meant.

Burned into the stranger's palm was his own mark. I didn't need a closer look to know that his would be an exact match for mine; forming a matching pair.

A soulmark.

But that... that's not possible.

It was a mark that formed between two wolf shifters, the first time they touched. It was the mark that revealed their soulmate.

A wolf's mate went deeper than marriage. It was a blessing bestowed by the moon goddess. It was a blessing that was only bestowed once. The mark revealed the other half of one's soul. The one you'd find most attractive. The one person you'd have the best chance of having children with. One's true equal.

But it was something only ever found between wolves...

Was this the sign that I'd been waiting for? Was this a sign that I was going to become a wolf?

I tensed my palm, trying to bring on the change. To have claws burst through my fingertips like I'd seen happen hundreds of times to my parents and siblings. My palm remained a stubborn and rather tense human hand. No. I still wasn't a wolf.

But how could I have a soulmate, if I wasn't able to shift?

Sparking was something that girls giggled over in classes, talking about how the first thing they would do after shifting into a wolf would be to shake hands with the most handsome alphas. But in all the time I've spent fantasizing about reaching my destiny and finally meeting my wolf, I somehow gave no thought to the whole issue of soulbounds and mates. That had always seemed like a concern for another day.

Not so much now, when the back of my palm and part of my arm had a marking the size of a teacup flaring across my skin in distinctive eddies and swirls.

The shifter I had sparked with was a boulder of a man. All thick muscles and a jawline sharp enough to cut through steel. Now staring at his palm, holding himself so rigidly, he didn't even seem to be breathing at all.

…This was not at all part of the plan.

It wasn't going to take him long at all to realize that something was wrong. Of course, he'd be expecting that he'd be bonding to his wolf's mate. Hopefully, he wasn't one of those arrogant wolves who thought of mere humans as pitiful nuisances. Some wolves refused to even speak to humans.

"I-I." I braced myself. To explain that I was not a wolf… yet. To explain that I had always felt something wild within myself. Prowling just beneath the surface. That I was sure that I was a late bloomer, if he would just give me enough time. That I still had two weeks before becoming effectively too old to be a shifter.

But that was all of the incoherent mumbling I managed to utter, before my mate opened his mouth to speak.

"No. No, that's not possible." The man looked upon the mark burnt onto his skin in absolute horror.

The rest of my words fell somewhere into a pit in the bottom of my stomach, along with any desire I might have had to get to know this man any better.

I didn't care if he was supposed to be my mate, or whatever this was. If that look of horror was what the moon goddess thought was the best match for me, then the moon goddess was wrong. I had to bear looks and judgements for my human status. I knew that everyone expected more from me—but there was no way I'd accept that attitude from a man who was supposed to be my lover.

I couldn't stop myself from rolling my eyes.

Brushing off the sticks and little rocks that clung aggressively to my gown, I checked to make sure I looked properly put together.

Great. Now that that was all sorted.

I gave the man, who must be a wolf shifter, a hard look.

There was no way in hell I was going to let this get to me—he simply wasn't worth it. I just had to get ahead of this.

"I accept your rejection." I told him once he met my gaze.

Flicking my hair to get the curled tresses out of my face, I strode off in the direction of the castle, without giving him another moment of my time.

I didn't need a soulmate, and I certainly didn't need one that clearly didn't want to be with me.

CHAPTER 2

ASHER

They called me the dark wolf.

None dared say it anywhere near me. But my wolf's senses were strong, and I could hear their conversations whether or not they wanted me listening. Over the past century, I'd heard all the rumors about myself. I'd heard how they warned new shifters to stay out of my way. Wondered if I was rabid. If the shifting burnt away just enough of the disease to make me appear sane. Called me borderline feral, and the pack's lone wolf.

The others were happy to believe that my heart was made of coal as black as the pitch fur of my wolf, but they didn't know my secret.

Stepping out of the shadows when I couldn't scent any other wolves for miles, I walked down a familiar trail. I'd taken it a dozen times before. Every decade or so. I did it, even as I knew it was ridiculous.

That didn't stop me from slinking away to the wishing well unseen, opening my palm and pouring out all the desire in my soul.

All to find my mate.

I was getting tired of solitude. Of being bound and helpless to the whims of fate. I couldn't do nothing. The powerlessness of it grated at me.

She walked straight into me and toppled backwards into the dirt. Dark wavy hair flying all askew. Her formal gown and heels—*who walked through the woods in high heels?*—all scratched up and stained.

Reflexively, I reached for her, gripping her hand, just to feel the electricity burn through me. The energy burst across my skin, blooming outwards in an intense flash of light. Lines spread from the point of contact with her skin, swirling and forming patterns.

In a sharp heat that I could feel all the way into my bones.

A soulmark.

This sparking was the exact moment I'd waited decades for. The very same event that brought me again and again here on the path to the wishing well.

After waiting for so long, it didn't seem real.

I stared.

The anger that pulsed through me, always just beneath the surface, was frozen away.

Numb.

It was as if I was staring at someone else's arm that was rudely attached to me.

I knew what the patterns were meant to look like. I'd always been drawn to the marks of mated wolves. Studying them surreptitiously whenever they bared an arm or shoulder near me.

Soulmarks looped in circular patterns. Within them all the phases of the moon were visible.

I knew almost immediately—something was wrong with my marks.

Examining each swirl, the flow of lines. My gaze traced over every line burnt into my skin, determined to uncover the source of the flaws.

Rather than forming complete patterns, ending in signature crescents and lines that curled in the phases of the moon—our lines faded into nothing. The connection, the bond, was somehow incomplete.

My wolf slept within me, barely paying attention to the events going around. He was not acting at all like the feral beast that had discovered his mate.

The soul connection between the wolves was corrupted somehow.

I'd always wondered if something within me was broken. But to see the proof of it etched permanently onto my own flesh—it was too much.

"No." Every wolf was meant to have a soulmate. Even the dark wolf. The rumors that I was meant to be a lone beast weren't real. "No, that's not possible."

My eyes snapped up at the sound of an irritated huff.

The girl who'd walked straight into me—my soulmate —she rolled her eyes, getting to her feet.

She glared at me with heat in her eyes, the fire in them simmering close to the surface. I could feel her fury. Without realizing it, I'd managed to piss her off.

"I accept your rejection." Her voice was cold. Rational and emotionless. She lifted her chin and walked away from me without a single word.

What? When had I rejected her?

Something in my stomach clenched tight.

No. I refused to believe that my soulmate would just reject me off the bat. She didn't even seem scared of me, like the others. What the hell just happened? What had I said when I'd noticed the incomplete mark? *No, that's not possible.*

Fuck.

The girl I'd waited decades for was pissed at me, before I'd ever said a single word to her. Stomping off as best as she was able to in her pointy heels.

Somehow, none of these turns of events surprised me.

At least her footwear made her dramatic escape rather slow.

I caught up to her, pausing. What was her name? I couldn't quite put my finger on who she was exactly. I grasped her shoulders, halting her. "We should talk about this."

"There's nothing to talk about." She refused to look at me.

I grasped her hand and a pulse of energy resonated through me—energy that felt familiar, drawing me in like a magnetic attraction.

"Look at the mark." I traced against the lines of her soulbond, brushing against buttery soft skin. "Do you see how the circular patterns stop here? That's not right, they are meant to connect back together. These marks were left unfinished."

Her markings as well as mine stopped abruptly, as if the well had run out of ink halfway through.

The woman sighed and brought her palm closer to her face. As if proximity would help clear up the confusion.

"Huh. So you're right." She cocked her head, looking at the mark from a different angle.

"That's why I said that this isn't possible. The connection is unfinished somehow."

She held her soul-marked palm jauntily at her hip. "I'm

supposed to believe that even though you have never had a soulmark before, you are somehow an expert?"

"I've spent a lot of time looking at soulmarks." I didn't want to get into the specifics of how long it had been. The girl seemed young, and I wasn't ready to scare her off... again.

She looked up at me skeptically. "So you didn't look at your arm in horror because I'm not a wolf?"

"You're not a... what?"

She wasn't a wolf?

That wasn't...

Her scent was floral, rose petals and pine needles. Lovely.

But wolves smelled like the forest. Pungent and wild. I couldn't scent even the faintest trace of wolf on her.

Gazing into her bright eyes was gazing into an impossibility. If I hadn't been staring directly at her mark, I'd refuse to believe it possible for a human to bear the soulmark. That she could be human, and be my mate.

Soulmates were only between wolves.

There was a good reason for that.

A connection between the wolves ensured that the beasts within were on their best behavior. My own wolf could be... temperamental. He sometimes viewed human women, not as a potential partner but rather as something to eat.

Shifting tore apart and reset bodies, which was what extended our lives. I'd already lived longer than a full human lifespan. Alone. All of the humans I'd cared about were long buried.

But more important than any of that. When shifting reset the body, it allowed for healing. Wolves could be violent, could rip into enemies... into one another.

All a human mate could be counted on, was to grow old and die. To die and leave me stranded behind.

Apparently I was silent for too long, because the girl tried to shrug away from the grip that I still had on her. "Look, I understand. If you don't want to be my mate, we don't have to be mates. Plenty of soulmarked wolves make other arrangements."

The thought of other arrangements pierced through my murky thoughts like shards of ice.

I'd waited over a century for her, and now not even five minutes after sparking, my soulmate was suggesting that we part ways.

After tugging against my hold, with all the ferocity of a kitten, she gave up, her expression utterly exasperated. "Besides, there's already another guy I'm interested in."

A feral growl reverberated deep in my chest.

I released her, clenching my hands into fists, trying to force back the claws threatening to erupt through my fingertips.

"If he touches you, I'll rip out his throat."

She sighed deeply, as if I was a boorish dinner companion she had the misfortune to be forced to sit next to. "Does that mean that you accept the bond with someone who's not a wolf?"

I opened my mouth to agree. To say yes. She was mine.

The reality of our situation pierced through the last shreds of my hope. Shattering any illusions that our relationship could ever work out.

This was what I wanted. All I wanted. For so fucking long.

She raised an eyebrow at me, waiting. After a moment she looked away. But not before I saw a flash of hurt in her eyes. "That's what I thought," she replied in a soft voice.

Something within me broke apart at the pain in her voice. Why the fuck did I have to be the cause of it?

None of this was her fault. Not that I could tell her that.

If I was stronger. If I had more control, things could be different.

But a human? With a wolf like me?

She straightened her posture, and her expression hardened, as she met my gaze once more. "If you aren't interested in me as a soulmate then you have no right to interfere in my life."

Not interested?

The girl was luscious. All generous curves over an athletic build. Round hips and an hourglass shape. I wanted to run my hands over every inch of her body. To tear open the exquisite fabric of her formal dining gown and learn the exact shape and color of her nipples.

I knew exactly what I could do to her. What my claws and teeth were capable of.

Humans couldn't heal themselves. Not in the way that shifters could.

It was the height of selfishness to entertain the idea of trying to make it work. But I refused to just give up. Not without a fight. Even if that fight was with my own damn self.

"I just need time to think."

"Why should I give you anything?" She scoffed.

"You probably shouldn't." There was no probably about it. The best thing for this girl would be to stay far, far from me. "But I'm asking for it anyway."

"Fine." She moved out of my grasp, heading back down the wishing trail. Her shapely hips swayed as she walked further and further away from me. "You have two weeks."

She was everything that I ever wanted. An impossibility.

Even now, the baser part of me whispered that it couldn't hurt.

Seduce her.

Press her against the trees and take her.

Make her scream my name.

Coat the inside of her sweet pussy. Drench her in my scent.

Claim her.

She was mine.

I couldn't listen to any of that.

There was no way I could be with a human girl so soft and lovely. No matter what I wanted.

I would break her.

CHAPTER 3
JENNY

Not even my stupid mate wanted me.

It was fine.

No, really. It was fine.

It's not like I was looking for a mate anyway.

I know that it's something that most girls swoon over and talk about. Some girls want to be wolves mainly for the chance to find their soulmate. Discussing how they are going to initiate that spark for the first time. Keeping track of which of the wolves were still single.

I was never interested in any of that.

I was more interested in reaching out to that strength I know was hidden within me. Tapping into the power of the wolf. I wanted to unleash her. Run through the forest with her. I could practically feel her presence within me, hidden beneath the surface.

But now rather than the sleek wildness of the wolf, I had to deal with a lumbering idiot who needed time to figure out if he wanted me. I should have laughed in his face.

I hadn't even bothered to learn his name, and he sure didn't ask for mine.

I guess he was handsome. He was masculine. Dark hair. Chiseled jaw. Rugged, and fierce. But his brawny physique was not the type of useless muscles that were aesthetically pleasing. No. His body was battle-hardened. If the shifter abilities didn't reform his skin, hiding away any but the worst injuries, he would be covered from the scars from dozens or even hundreds of battles. Instead of showing up on his skin, it was visible in hints and shadows in his eyes.

He was almost the sort of wolf that girls drool over. He exuded the quiet authority of an alpha. I would be shocked if he wasn't at least a high-ranking beta. Except that he was a little too rough around the edges. Getting close to him would be a little like getting too close to a wildfire. The heat wasn't comforting as much as it was unclaimed. Out of control.

I didn't notice him again, until I went to the formal dinner. As soon as I saw him sitting with his formal wear, I couldn't imagine how I had missed him before. In his dinner suit, he seemed even more formidable in a dark navy suit with golden lapels, stretched tight over a wide muscular frame. Larger than life. My would-be-mate sat at the high table. The table reserved for the alpha's immediate family and the high generals. So my first instincts were right. The man was an alpha. One of the most powerful men in the castle. Obviously he wouldn't want to mess around with a woman who wasn't able to shift.

Could this be a sign that I was going to shift? It had to be. How else would I have a soulmate with a wolf?

But there was the matter with the incomplete soulmark. Just like everything else involving my fate, it was incomplete. An unknown. If I had ever wanted a mate and all that, this would be the sort of thing that would make me inconsolable.

I sat next to my brother, Nels, who was eating his meal as if he was a millisecond away from shifting into a wolf and tearing into his meat, just gripping it tight in his fingers and tearing into it with his fangs.

I held in a sigh. Wolves were really afforded all the grace. My older brother and even my younger sister were more than free to eat like uncivilized heathens. But then again, both of them were shifters. Their behavior was tolerated. Even expected to a certain extent.

I was afforded no such consideration. I sat at my seat, holding my silverware almost primly, though I longed for the freedom to just tear at my food like a common barbarian. Like I was nothing but a primal beast rather than a lady.

It was difficult to get Nels' attention. In his defense, dinner was quite good tonight. The garlic and honey glazed chicken paired with sweet potatoes was particularly well seasoned. I had to tap Nels' elbow three times before I could take his eyes away from his plate.

"Hey."

"Hey yourself." Nels replied with a mouth full of honey glazed poultry.

"Can you tell me the name of that shifter at the high table? Third from the end."

Nels smirked, looking up from his plate. "Don't tell me that you're dating the wolves now." He scanned the room, when his gaze locked on my mate. "Uhhh... you're not actually interested in Asher Rasmussen? I mean, he is a dominant wolf without a mate. But he's not the type to go for non-shifters."

"Don't call me that."

"What? A non-shifter? Why? That's what you are."

I pursed my lips, but said nothing.

Nels ripped off another hunk of chicken, chewing thoughtfully. "I thought that you were interested in that other guy? The soldier?"

"I am. But it's complicated."

"Why? Because of Rasmussen? Didn't think that you were one of those alpha chasers."

"Goddess, no. I'm not chasing after him. I just wanted to know his name."

"Then who are you planning on taking to the ball?"

I bit the inside of my lip. Hard. This was one of those incidents where I wish that it was socially acceptable for me to react like one of the shifters. It would really let off some steam if I could smash a cup or howl in annoyance. But no, I had to keep my cool.

The winter solstice ball. How had I forgotten? Father told me weeks ago that he expected me to be in attendance this time.

Damn it.

"I have time to figure it out. The ball isn't until a couple weeks out." There was the little problem that I had told Asher that I was going to give him two weeks. How do I ask someone out to the ball when I had already promised my hulking brooding jerk of a mate that I was going to give him time? It wasn't like I could ask Asher anyway; he didn't even want to be with me.

Inspiration struck. While I did have to attend this awful

ball, I did not have to go with a real date. "I could just ask Fredrik to go with me as a friend."

Nels snorted at me. "He asked Helga out weeks ago. Also it's not a couple weeks out. The ball is next week."

Wait, *what?*

I had to figure all of this out—the date and the dress. Oh, and also the general path and scope of my entire life that will inevitably be shaped by the decision that I make for this awful ball. All in less than a week?

I had to figure out how to become a shifter! I didn't have time for all of this.

"Fine, then I'll just go with you." I took a triumphant bite of chicken, glad to have gotten this mess squared away.

But Nels shook his head. "Claire already asked me."

Damn my little sister for being organized. She beat me to it.

"You're killing me Nels."

"She asked me weeks ago. 'Sides, people sort of expect shifters to go with family and friends, because of the whole sparking thing." He stared at me sideways, frowning. As if to say, that it was alright for him and Claire to do it. Them. The wolf shifters in the family could get away with passing on real dates. But what in the world was I doing? I was supposed to be able to date whoever I wanted without consequence, without having to worry about soulbonding. So why wasn't I trying to find a date?

Except that I already had a soulbond. Sort of.

Even if it was an incomplete one, with none of the undying love and acknowledgement that this was the other half of my soul, to go with it.

"Why don't you ask your soldier to go with you as a friend?"

I sighed. Why disappoint one man, when I could disappoint two? I could just friendzone the man I'd been pining after all year and piss off my mate all in one go. "That would just complicate things."

Nels smirked. A bit of mischief lurking behind his emerald eyes. "So what? Then complicate things."

CHAPTER 4
ASHER

My attention was immediately drawn to the girl, as soon as she arrived at the dining hall. Lit by candlelight, she was breathtaking. Dark hair flowed down to the middle of her back in waves. Fine arched brows, over eyes that were bright, and flashed with intelligence. Graceful high cheekbones and full red lips.

Poise and strength clung to her athletic build. She was the sort of woman that everyone should be drooling over. Fighting to claim. Here I was, doing nothing as she ignored me. As she strode to the table filled with high level betas, without looking at me once.

She was beautiful—and she hated me.

Then she went and sat next to a man who was far too attractive. Curly brown hair. Green eyes taken straight out of a fucking fairy tale. He smiled at her far too easily. The two of them hunched close and whispered to each other conspiratorially.

Rage was itching under my skin. Under the table, my claws burst through my fingertips. I dug them into the wood under the table, letting the solid press of wood ground me. As if something as simple as a table would be enough to hold back the beast within me.

I would decorate the crystal chandeliers with his intestines. Open him up and let everyone see that he wasn't worthy of her.

Did she not take me seriously, when I told her that I'd rip out the throat of any man that touched her? Did she really think it was a good idea to blatantly flirt with another shifter, right in front of me?

"Do I need to help you kill someone? Or help hold you back?" Harald, my cousin, asked in a low voice. He was my closest relative, still living.

"What's his name?" I held my wolf back, enough to speak. He prowled within me, tasting a chase in the air. But he knew enough to wait for the human side. To get the information needed to hunt. "The shifter with the beige overcoat with bronze lapels?"

Harald quickly scanned through the dining hall, until his gaze fell on the pretty boy. "That's Nels Kolbeck. He's Rune's son. A fairly reliable shifter."

I snorted. Reliable. "How reliable is he if he's unmated and chasing after women during dinner?"

Harald simply frowned. "Chasing after... he's not flirting with anyone."

Was my cousin blind? Could he not see this Nels fellow hunched over and whispering to *her*.

She wasn't his to flirt with. Wasn't his mate.

Not that she was mine either.

Something ugly rose to the surface within me. The part of me that just wanted to claim her, consequences be damned. To do it now. In front of everyone.

It wasn't even the wolf whispering within me, but something dark. Something out of control. Something that wanted to reach her and rip her away from the man who dared to sit so close to her. To breathe the air that belonged to her and her alone. To take in her sweet floral scent that didn't have a trace of me on it. And fix that.

The girl was right. If I didn't acknowledge this bond between us, I had no right to her. I couldn't ignore our bond and expect a woman so lovely to remain single for the rest of her life.

Harald must have noted the barely restrained rage that I was trying and failing to force behind my regular stoic exterior.

"You mean that girl he's talking to? That's Nels' sister."

All the tension seeped out of me like water slipping out of a leaking bucket. I had gotten this all wrong.

Harald raised one eyebrow at my change in expression. "The Kolbeck siblings are all rather attractive. I know at least one wolf who went out of his way to attend Jenny's coming of age ceremony. But she never did end up as a shifter. Shame about that one. She's from a strong bloodline, and a prestigious line of wolves. Pretty. But she never shifted. Nothing but a human."

I watched her in my peripheral vision. Now that I knew that there wasn't another man trying to tear her away from me, I could better appreciate how animated she was. How at ease. The quick and delighted smiles she threw at her brother.

Harald cocked his head at me as if I was a puzzle that he was trying to solve. "You want her?"

I jerked like he'd struck me. Was desire written all over my face? Was I that obvious? I had to pull myself together.

"Like you said, she's human." I tried to keep the bitterness out of my voice.

Jenny.

She had all the qualities that were absolutely perfect in a mate. Beautiful and strong, with a flash of intelligence in her eyes. There was something bold about her. The way that she had stood up to me in the forest. She wasn't a girl who ever let anyone give her any shit. She glared at me as if I was a disobedient lapdog and not a shifter capable of ripping apart the table between us if it came to that.

She had every quality I wanted, except for the one I hadn't even considered. The one I took for granted.

Harald cleared his throat. "What about that ball that's coming up? Why not invite her?"

I shook my head in disbelief. "You're encouraging me to pursue a human?"

"What's it going to hurt if you go dance with a pretty girl?"

"It wouldn't be me getting hurt." I couldn't relax. The sharp tang of cortisol hung in the air. I took a deep breath, as I tried and failed to bring about the control that the other wolves seemed to master with ease.

I went very still, like a prey animal. Like the lack of motion would help me elude the memory. Of another lovely face. Pale. With just a trickle of blood flowing from her lips. Looking so alive, besides the gash that had torn her open.

Ripped her so deep that nothing could stitch her back together again.

Humans were just so soft.

Just bustling along all their short little lives, with no idea of all the dangers lurking beneath the surface. How very thin the line was for them. Between living and dying.

Breathing and stillness. Sweet laughter… dances at a ball… and oblivion.

When one swipe of a claw could drag them all the way to the other side.

Harald was silent for long enough that I thought that was the end of it. He'd known me longer than most anyone. Long enough to watch me lose every last human I'd been close to. Only a handful were from old age.

He leaned in closer and spoke in a voice so low that even another wolf would have trouble listening in with all the pervasive noise in the dining hall. "If you are serious about her, talk to the General."

I didn't need to ask about which general. There was only one who had earned that title. I wasn't the oldest wolf in the pack by far. There were wolves brushing close to a full millennium. But I was one of the older dominant wolves. Even our last alpha had handed the mantle down to his son and passed away not even a decade after.

Not all of the gamma and beta wolves had seen bloodshed. Not all of them paid for the protection of the pack. Paid with injuries that didn't scar wolf flesh, but pierced us nevertheless.

While there were many wolves older than I, there were far fewer who were more dominant than me. Because hierarchy was maintained in violence and bloodshed.

The General was the oldest of them.

"Why would you think I'm serious about her?" I refused to look at the girl full on, though I tracked every move she made out of the corner of my eyes.

"I haven't seen you look at anyone. Not in decades." Harald smiled. It didn't quite reach his eyes.

"It's been a while." I was forced to admit.

The problem wasn't that I couldn't love a human. The problem was that I had.

It all ended in gruesome pain.

Someone innocent. Someone who was never built as a host for the beasts that prowled beneath our skins. They should stay as far as possible from those claws and fangs.

They were never made to endure our violence.

CHAPTER 5
JENNY

"Do you think that this color is a bit much?" I pouted my red, red lips together, inspecting the effect in the brass mirror above my vanity. I usually went for more subtle pinks, but I couldn't help but admit that the red was a more sophisticated hue.

Trisha paused in the middle of braiding my hair. She was working her magic on my pearl pins, arranging them in my hair like constellations. "It's gorgeous. What's the problem?"

"I'm asking Jayden out as a friend." I pouted. Why had I let my brother talk me into this? Jayden was going to get the wrong idea once I told him that I only wanted to go out as friends. There was a smaller chance that Asher was going to get the wrong idea as well.

It didn't seem like the shifter cared. At least not enough to actually invite me to the ball. No. There was no way that a high and mighty shifter warrior could ever deign to ask the little human girl to the dance. The problem would come if Asher decided to take offense to me taking another man out to the ball.

Didn't he tell me that he would harm any man who touched me? Did he expect for me to go the rest of my life without being touched then?

The fact remained that I had to find a date to the dance.

Which put me into an impossible situation. There was no pleasing everyone. My father had practically ordered me to go. He must have considered finding a date to be like moving on from my "unhealthy obsession" with being a wolf. If I wasn't a shifter, I was at liberty to date whoever I wanted, without worrying about a pesky soulmate out there. Waiting for me. That would have all been fine. Before I sparked an incomplete soulbond.

But if Asher didn't want to ask me to the dance that was his own problem, and he could just deal with the consequences.

Trisha tsked as she fastened another pin. She'd been working for my family since I was a little girl, and knew all about my love life. Or rather, my lack of a love life. "Then ask him as your date. I've seen the way that boy looks at you. He's more than *interested*. Though, honestly, anyone would be lucky to go to the dance with you."

I sighed. I'd originally planned on asking Jayden as my date to this ball. If I had to go, I should be able to enjoy it somewhat. Jayden wasn't as dominant and brawny as Asher, but he was nice to look at. More importantly, he didn't hate me for something I couldn't control. For being human.

That's just for now. I'm going to show all of them that they are wrong about me. I can feel a wolf inside of me. I know that she's there.

It wasn't always stated, but even among the wolves, things didn't always work out with soulmates. Sometimes they had to work out other arrangements. Sometimes they even married other people, for political reasons. Or because they hadn't found anyone for too long and ended up marrying elsewhere.

Even though the majority of wolves behaved like my siblings did. Waiting to spark with their soulmates. Avoiding dating. Not finding the potential conflict of interests worth it. Not wanting to find their soulmate when it was already too late.

Well my soulmate didn't seem like he was going to be my problem for much longer. If we ended up being one of those cases that ended up as a cautionary tale for everyone else, well, that was fine by me.

My hand hovered over my handkerchief as I toyed with the idea of brushing off the red lipstick, before dropping it.

My pointed heels clattered against the stone slabs outside, on my way to the courtyard, but the sound was soon swallowed up by the clash of swords, as metal struck against metal. Soldiers practiced their elaborate routines with longswords. Some drilled their parrying and footwork, while others dueled with partners.

Though I was technically human, something in me shied away from the glint and flash of metal; they were practicing with silver. The weapons were refined by human artisans, and stored carefully under lock and key. They were a necessary evil. In the event of an enemy pack of wolves who tried to infiltrate our territory, we had to be prepared.

As I was still human, I could still touch all metals. But as soon as the wolf emerged within me, she would be overpowered by silver—it was all the power of the moon. But rather than being dulled by the vastness of space, all of that silver brought the power of the moon too close for shifters to handle.

Just one touch would burn the wolf.

As I approached, one soldier called off his duel and headed over.

A soldier built straight out of a dream. Tall, with the sleek build of a swimmer. Sharp jawline. Clear blue eyes set in a handsome face. His light brown hair was wavy in a way that suggested his hair would be curly if he let it grow out.

I looked up into his tall frame as he smiled in greeting. "Hey stranger, what brings you all the way out here? Talking with us lowly soldiers."

"I am being forced to socialize, against my will. To attend the winter solstice ball."

"What a tragedy," Jayden smiled, leaning closer. Close enough for me to see his dimples. "Whatever shall you do?"

"I thought I might go ask one of the soldiers if they would be so kind as to accompany me. Do you know any man up to the task of protecting me from all the tedium and pomp of a formal dance?"

"It's a date then." Jayden smiled wider, his gaze dipping down and lingering on the red of my lipstick.

"Not a date." I smiled in reply, to soften the blow. "I'm merely allowing you to rescue me from the tyranny of forced social interaction."

"No woman should have to suffer through tyranny. Not under my watch." Jayden's easy grin was undeterred. Did he think that I was merely playing hard to get?

His panty-melting smirk did not get the message that we weren't going to the ball together as a date. I could have firmly corrected him, but I liked the heat in his eyes as he stared at me. I like how he looked at me with a promise of more to come.

His attention was dangerous; it could end up annoying all the wrong people.

I couldn't quite bring myself to care.

CHAPTER 6
ASHER

I couldn't get my fucking head together.

Every wolf shifter has a soulmate once in their life.

I stupidly believed that all my problems would go away once I found her.

I was only a few days into the two weeks she'd given me to figure out what the hell I wanted, and was no closer to giving my answer.

I'm an alpha. The pack needs me. Needs my strength. So what if I'm alone. Who gives a shit?

If I had any decency left in my body, I would have rejected her the moment I learned what she was.

But something in my blood sang whenever she was near. Something that had me seeking her out, watching her from the shadows. Something that burned through my veins. That curved around my claws, itching to burst out and hunt her down.

Something that went straight to my cock, making me harder than I'd ever been in my life.

She was my soulmate, and there was nothing stopping

me. Nothing but my own thoughts that were spiraling so hard out of control that I was dizzy with it.

My soulmate was fucking here. The moon goddess had burnt my soulmark into her skin. There would be no easier task in the world than to go to her. To give in.

It wasn't that simple.

I wanted her.

I wanted that tight body. I wanted those rosebud lips.

I wanted the spark of fire in her eyes, her wit.

But more than I wanted her, I wanted her whole.

And for that to happen I had to stay the fuck away.

My thoughts were suffocating me. The walls of the castle, restricting. Holding me in. I had to get out.

Jogging out the arched doorway, I headed down the paths leading to old growth forest, with vegetation thick enough to dampen the bustle of human activity.

I stripped to my skin, and unleashed the dark wolf.

My jaws cracked as they lengthened, fangs erupting, piercing through my gums. Stretching and breaking through skin. Bones shifted, twisting into the part of me that was feral. Dominant and unconquered. Until every inch of me was coated with a pelt black as a starless night sky.

My paws hit the forest floor, tearing across the earth.

The dark beast was built for killing and fucking. Tonight, I'd be an instrument of death. A grim reaper for any forest creature that drew the attention of the hunt. All I could do was hope I'd run into something strong enough to distract him. I couldn't satisfy all of his needs in blood forever.

THE GENERAL no longer resided in the castle proper. The entrance to his rooms was through a portcullis fortified for war.

When I knocked, the General ripped the door open, claws extended. The air was thick with the acidic stench of cortisol and adrenaline. When he saw me, the General allowed the wolf to leer out, inhaling the air, inhaling the pack bond in my blood, before he stepped aside to let me pass.

But there was no iron hint in the air as his claws retreated back into his skin. He kept them out, still on alert.

His room was sparse, organized with a military precision. Laid out a coffee table with intricate woodwork, was a set of weapons. A cudgel, chain mace, dagger—it seemed as if I interrupted him from sharpening it.

He didn't invite me to sit, or dispense with any of the niceties. Instead he nodded and waited.

I didn't know how to put my question into words, so I unbuttoned my gloves, exposing the skin on my palm. Showing him my mark. The electric burns were healed into black swirls and eddies. But rather than flowing into all of the phases of the moon, my marks stopped abruptly.

Broken. Incomplete.

The General cocked his head in a motion that was more animal than man. His nostrils flared.

If my mate had been a wolf. If I had allowed myself to give in. Allowed myself to seduce her. Taken her. He would have been able to scent exactly who she was.

Now, the only thing to smell on my flesh was a faint

trace of burning from when the mark was etched into me permanently.

The General looked me in the eyes, in a silent demand.

I could tell what he wanted to know as if he'd spoken the words out loud.

Who is she?

As my eyes traced the path of my soulmark, my mind wandered to flowing dark hair. With my hand woven through her long locks, holding her in place. At the right angle to watch as I pushed into her body. As I marked her with my scent as fully as she'd been marked by my soulbond. Drenching her in enough of my wolf aroma, that it wouldn't matter what she was. None of the others would dare get close enough to her to find out. "She's human."

The General shook his head. "She can't be."

"But she is. My mate has never shifted. With my soulmark burned into my arm, my wolf remained fully asleep. Wasn't interested at all."

"After eight hundred years, it isn't every day when I see something new. Never seen this before." The General drummed his claws against the counter. The myriad scratches in the wood suggested that this was a common occurrence. "Has not having a wolf connection impacted your human relationship?"

"I'm not sure." My answer wasn't good enough. The General looked me square in the eyes, silently demanding more. To know the truth. I admitted, "We don't have a relationship."

The General snorted, shaking his head at me. "Well, why haven't you taken her? She's still your mate."

"How can I? She's human." Irritation colored my words.

The General stiffened, tilting his head at me as if to

examine me closer. As if he was seeing me now for the first time. "You didn't strike me as the type to reject your mate."

"But I don't have a choice." I clenched my hands tight, pressing my fist into my thigh. Holding back the waves of anger demanding that I transform. That I go after this threat to my well being.

Too bad that the person threatening my happiness was myself.

The General sighed heavily. "The moon goddess only gives the soulbond once. If you don't want your mate then you don't get one."

The finality in his tone grated at me. "It's not that simple. I want her... but she's human. If I can't guarantee that she's going to be alright, it isn't worth taking the chance."

"That might be the stupidest thing I've heard anyone say. Even if your mate was able to shift, nothing is guaranteed." The General said the words with a cold and crisp matter of factness.

A thought dropped into the pit of my stomach. Making it tense with understanding. He was talking from experience. The General had been alone for centuries. *What had happened to his mate?*

"But, my wolf...he can get aggressive..." I didn't want to get into specifics about how my wolf had stalked down humans. How hard it had been to reign him in. It was worse after my time on the battlefield. He'd acquired a taste for killing. No other living being gave quite the same challenge, as ripping apart a man.

"Your mate would spend more time among the wolves. But besides that, its just the same as fucking any other human."

I didn't have anything to say to that.

I didn't have to. The General found his answer in my silence. He scoffed, incredulously. "You've never fucked a human? How old are you? Eighty?"

"A hundred and twenty seven."

He stared at me as if I'd unexpectedly grown a second head.

I grit my teeth, needing to defend myself. I wasn't like one of those wolves that went around trash-talking humans. The kind that acted repulsed when they were forced to interact with non-shifters in pleasant society. No. I had a real reason to hold back from my mate. "My wolf picked up a taste for killing in the war. Why would the moon goddess give me a human girl when I have a wolf that might tear her to pieces?"

The General stared at me in disgust. As if he was completely done with my shit. He strode to his door, unlatching it. Motioning me to walk through it. "I'm not the person to discuss the workings of the moon goddess. Go find a priest if you want to fucking do that. Stop wasting my time."

CHAPTER 7

JENNY

The great hall looked completely unrecognizable. The golden leaf glinted off crown molding. Garlands of wisteria created a flowery canopy, under which flutes clinked and champagne flowed.

The colors seemed brighter. Surrounded by the warm glow of candlelight, and the scintillation of crystal chandeliers. As the humans mingled among the wolves, all dressed in their best attire. Women fluttered around in all the latest designs in silk, charmeuse and lace, like walking gems.

Claws were sheathed in only the finest velvet gloves. Fangs were hidden behind generous smiles. The beasts were out among the rest, and on their best behavior.

I could feel his eyes on me, even before I turned and met his gaze. The atmosphere suddenly felt weighed down. Tense, as if all the air around me was holding its collective breath. Taking a steadying breath, I turned to face him.

He seemed somehow taller in his charcoal tweed three-piece suit. With his tie done up in an Eldredge knot. The classy material did nothing to hold back the ferocity of his wolf, just as beautiful spots and stripes patterns did nothing to diminish the danger of the wild cats.

I could feel the fire in his gaze.

I knew exactly what he was seeing.

My dress was red silk, slit along the side revealing a hint of leg with each step. The dress clung to every curve, and lace accentuated all my best features. I was considering a more demure navy piece. Made of sturdier fabric that showed less skin.

Then I decided, fuck it.

Just because my mate wasn't interested, by no means meant that it was time for me to bundle up my sexuality, leave the castle and devote myself to a nunnery. If he didn't want me, that was his own damn problem.

Perhaps I'd miscalculated.

Asher looked like he'd been struck by an arrow. Every muscle in his body was tense.

From within the depths of his dark eyes, I could practically see the stars, as they locked on mine.

His jaw hung open as his nostrils flared wide. As he took in my scent. Breathing deep, like he couldn't get enough.

Slowly. With all the deadly power of a predator stalking down his next target, Asher prowled toward me.

I gulped slowly. Riveted to each step that drew him closer to me. A powerful man. His dominance had its own presence. It lured me in as if he had his own gravitational pull.

But the hand that clutched my elbow was not his.

"My dear, you look absolutely stunning." Jayden smiled too widely, completely unaware of the tension hanging thick between me and my mate—so thick, I was practically drowning in it.

I smiled back weakly. For a moment, I'd completely

forgotten that I'd even invited Jayden along as my not-a-date.

Now that he was leading me away from my mate, I wondered why I'd never even thought of coming to the ball solo. I forced myself not to look at Asher. Didn't need to look at him to tell that he was likely seething.

What was it that he said would happen if another man touched me? Something about ripping out something. I'd grown up listening to dominant wolves bickering all the time. But the dark look in Asher's eyes when Jayden took my arm... That told me that Asher meant every word that he said.

Jayden leaned in closer to me, and whispered. "Would you care to dance?"

"Don't lean so close." I hissed back. Keeping an ear out for a wolf growl. For heavy footsteps stomping over this way.

"Why not?" Jaden snorted.

"People might get the wrong idea." Well, people I couldn't care less about. The one I was worried about was more than just a person. Not that I was going to tell Jayden that.

"If your problem is what people might see, then I have a solution for that."

I huffed, holding back my barely contained frustration. I really should have made it clear to him that this wasn't a date.

I guess that after a year of flirting, these expectations were inevitable.

Jayden placed his hands low on my back as he gently guided me. I was already so tense, trying to keep the grinning idiot alive, that I didn't notice where he was taking me until we were already away from the festivities. He'd led me outside onto the balcony, shutting the door to the dance firmly behind him.

The moon was clear in the sky, framed by the arched pillars. She was in her fourth phase, waxing gibbous. Beautiful. She was my own personal ticking countdown. I only had a week left, and I hadn't even tried anything. I'd barely had any time for my strength building exercises. Even had to skip my daily morning jog. Twice. All because I had to stay up late getting last minute fittings on the dress. I promised myself that I'd dedicate more time to my wolf etiquette readings, but found that time eaten up instead by manicure appointments. Taking Claire out shopping, as she'd shifted in her last formal dress, destroying it. Even though she'd complained through the four hours of alterations, and had to sit through them all over again.

All of my free time had all been taken up by this stupid ball.

The chill in the night air curved around my shoulders, seeping through the thin fabric of my dress. I hadn't brought a shawl because that would ruin the lines of the dress. Obviously.

A shiver trailed down the length of my spine as the winter cold pierced me.

"Cold?" Jayden murmured. "I could keep you warm."

Suddenly he was too close. Slouched against the pillar at my side, he reached for my cheek, holding me in place. Leaning in.

"Jayden, stop it." I pulled away. Rolling my shoulders, as if I could brush off all the frustration of the night along with it.

But instead of stopping, he pressed even closer. Backing me into the cold stone of the pillar, his face looming closer, eyes half-hooded.

What the hell did he think he was doing?

It was like he didn't even realize that there was an entire castle of wolf shifters that could hear us. All I had to do was yell for Nels, and he'd come charging out here.

"Stop it." I pressed against his chest to push Jayden off. Needing some space. Annoyed enough at this entire affair to storm back to my rooms without even having a single dance.

He didn't listen. Instead he held me tighter.

"Relax. You'll like this."

That was the only warning I got before he slammed his thin lips greedily against mine.

I gasped in shock, and Jayden took that as an invitation to plunge his tongue into me. Groaning, as he began to overtly thrust his tongue around my mouth as if he were trying to fuck me with it.

His other hand was busy roaming around my body, grasping my ass hard.

I tried to pull away from him. Had to break free from those persistent lips before things got even more out of hand. Had to call for Nels, or hell for Claire—even if she'd be pissed about ruining another dress rescuing me.

I just couldn't pull away. His lips followed mine no matter which way I turned.

Jayden was so distracted that he didn't even notice the danger looming closer, as Asher stepped out of the shadows, heading towards us.

CHAPTER 8
ASHER

The soldier was a dead man the second he touched my mate. Clouding the air with the stench of his lust. Eyeing her, as if a pathetic worm like him, deserved to stand in the same room as her, much less put his foul little hands on her.

Did she really not see the way that he was just blatantly staring at her chest? Like she was a piece of meat?

I wanted to rip him apart.

Only one thing stopped me from smearing the dance floor with his blood and bile. From tearing him all the way open. It was the look of annoyance on my mate's face.

That's right, you little piece of shit. She doesn't want you.

Rage pulsed hot through my veins, until a haze covered everything in a film.

But I held myself perfectly still, watching as the soldier led my girl away.

There was something that I didn't like about the look on his face. Something was wrong. He was too quick to pull Jenny away, isolating her from the rest of the dancers.

A calm fury settled over me. There was no need to act irrationally. He'd be dead soon enough.

Decision made, I headed out. Taking the doorway with a balcony adjacent to the one the soldier led my mate through. Listening the entire time.

My mate only seemed annoyed with the man at first. I hurried when I heard her hiss at him. "Stop it."

When she had to say it a second time, cold hatred bloomed in my heart. I had no tolerance for a man who suddenly lost his ability to hear a woman when she said no.

Silently. I approached them. Reigning in my rage when I was close enough to see him put his hands all over my girl. Clutching at her breasts and ass as he shoved his filthy tongue halfway down her throat.

As my mate noticed me, her eyes widened. From her, I could smell sticky adrenaline. Fight or flight, not lust.

None of this was her fault. It wasn't as if she'd wanted this.

How fucking dare he? Who the fuck did he think he was? To touch any woman who told him to take his hands off of her.

But no.

This fucker didn't do this to any woman.

He touched mine.

Jenny was under my protection.

This sloppy excrement of a man should have known better. Even if he hadn't known that Jenny belonged to me, he should have known enough to realize that he wasn't deserving of her. Her noble status, the warriors in her bloodline, her pedigree was not for one such as him.

He didn't deserve to lick the dirt off the bottom of her high heels.

As soon as I reached the two of them, I grabbed the man by the throat. Wrenching him away from my mate.

Watched the emotions flit across his face. Indignation at being interrupted. Confusion. Then shocked recognition, bordering on panic.

Good.

I was glad that he recognized me. I wanted him to be afraid in his last moments. He should fear me. I wanted to wrench every last morsel of pain out of this pathetic coward's guts.

Not a quick death.

No.

I wanted him to suffer.

It was a shame that he wasn't a shifter. So I couldn't allow him to heal and prolong the experience.

I wanted to feel his blood well up under my claws, again and again and again.

"Asher!" Her voice pierced through the haze of violence that overshadowed and covered every inch of my brain. Coating my mind in rage.

My name on her lips, slightly high-pitched, sounded delightful. I wanted to give her more reasons to call out my name. I'd make her scream for me. I'd rip the pleasure out of her feeble human body. Make her take it.

"Asher, just let him go. This is all just a stupid misunderstanding."

Let him go? Her first words sounded appealing. Though it would end all too soon. I could let him go. Hold him over the edge of the balcony and let his body tumble to the earth below.

It was a kinder death than the man deserved. But I'd be lying if I couldn't admit that the thought of it fascinated me. I suddenly wanted to see it. What would the impact do to his pretty little face? Would he still look pretty with his body ripped open by the fall?

But then she had said that this was all just a misunderstanding.

That's where my little mate was wrong.

I don't know what she told this soldier, she was obviously annoyed at his behavior. I don't think that she expected him to kiss her.

But him?

Before the stink of fear clouded his judgment, his smell stank of excitement. Desire.

He wanted my mate. Wanted someone that was never supposed to be his.

"If you hurt him, it is just going to ruin the party for everyone." Her words were logical and clear. I would have thought that she was unaffected by all of this, if it weren't for the rising scent of her anxiety.

The man assaulted her—there would be no leniency. No negotiation.

But then again.

There was also no need to bother my mate with this. She'd gone through enough tonight. I wasn't going to be the one to make things worse for her.

I released my grip on the soldier's throat. Only for him to start sputtering, clutching at it and grasping at his neck.

I refrained from rolling my eyes. It was as if he'd never had his life threatened before. Pathetic.

When he stopped coughing, he bowed his head in a feeble attempt at wolf appeasing. Had this idiot even passed the lupine etiquette class? Did he really think that bending his head like that was by any means sufficient? It didn't even scratch the surface of what he'd need to make up for what he did. He should be on the ground *groveling*.

Not that a submissive posture would work on me. Now that I've seen exactly what he was.

"Sir, I had no idea that you were interested in this woman. I would have never... if I had known." His voice had turned high-pitched, and he was looking down at the balcony tile, averting his gaze from mine. The soldier turned sharply to Jenny rounding on her. "Why didn't you—"

"Turn your fucking face away from her. You don't get to talk to her." I cut him off.

He turned pale, looking away from Jenny as if she didn't exist. The soldier raised his hands, as if to show that he was unarmed, backing away slowly.

I made no sign that I noticed. No growl. Not one twitch of the claws that could cut through the thin skin of his neck. Quicker and easier than cutting through paper.

As soon as the man put enough distance between us, he exited out the balcony door. Making his escape without saying a single word.

Not that it mattered. I'd gotten his scent. He wasn't getting away from me.

But I had more important matters to attend to at the moment.

"Are you alright?" Heat flushed through my body as all of my muscles tensed, waiting on her response. If she was hurt... Fuck patience. I was going to go straight after him.

"Me?" Jenny cocked her head in surprise. "Yeah. I'm fine."

She shook her head, looking at the balcony door as if she could see through it to the dancers at the ball. As if she could track the progress of her ex-date as he moved further and further away from her.

I forced myself to heed her words. To let them sink into

my mind, ripping through my thoughts like a stone thrown into a pond.

She was fine.

A man had forced his attention on her.

Had I shown an iota of interest in her… even the soldier was smart enough to back the fuck away from her. He'd even admitted it to my face. I was the one stupid enough to leave her vulnerable. She was alone out in the world and ripe for the taking.

"I spent a year pining after him," Jenny shook her head. "Turns out he's terrible at kissing."

Terrible all round person. If Jenny hadn't stopped me, all that would be left of him would have been his stains on the floor.

"Well thank you for that." Jenny smoothed her hands along the sides of her dress. Her scent changed from the spiky scent of adrenaline, nervousness, to something much cooler.

The scent of her happiness fluttered through the party when she'd first arrived, mingling among the dancers at the ball. Then, her emotions were crisp and light, like vanilla in the air. Now the scent of her happy excitement had all but faded.

That asshole shouldn't be able to take another thing from Jenny.

I held out my hand to her. "Dance with me."

Jenny blinked in surprise at the proffered limb. Stared at it as if it were an exotic animal on display. As if looking at it long enough would make the limb sprout its own legs and run from her.

The corner of her lips twitched in amusement, as she laid her arm on top of mine.

We walked together to the dance floor. Eyes weren't

immediately locked on mine, but I noticed a few glances our way. People immediately turned their heads away when they realized I'd noticed their stares. It was subtle, but clear. They were aware of the two of us, walking together.

I hadn't danced for... I couldn't even remember how long it had been. Had successfully avoided it for decades. Hadn't ever taken a woman on a date out in public before.

Anyone paying attention would be wondering what I was doing with a human after all of this time. I've never had a reputation for flirting with humans. Or with anyone, really.

The two of us made our way to the dance floor.

We stuck out, amongst the other dancers on the floor—wolves with their soulmates, the humans with their dates. Subtly, the other dancers made way for us. There was a circle of curiosity, all around us, giving us space in the crowded hall. Not that I cared.

I couldn't take my eyes off of her. In that flowing dress. Silky. Luscious and red. Clinging to every one of her curves like a second skin. She was absolutely mouth-watering.

As the music began, I bowed to her. Without taking my eyes off hers for a single moment. The notes were sweet and lovely. The stringed instruments were crystal flutterings in the air. As the melody softly nudged me to hold her closer.

The steps came back to me, in muscle memory ingrained from my formative years. I waltzed without error. But my partner was an exceptional dancer. Her movements were fluid, smooth as flowing water. She made the dance look elegant. Refined.

Watching her made my throat go dry, as every inch of my body heated with want. She was so gorgeous. Fucking stunning.

As we bowed at the end of the dance, she stepped closer to me. "Can we talk?"

Her eyes were curious, not angry with me. Watching me like I was a puzzle, and it was her job to figure out what was going on.

In reply, I led her away from the dance floor, to a deserted table. On the way, I plucked two flutes of champagne, wordlessly offering her a glass. She sipped at it thoughtfully, as she took a seat next to me.

"What's all this about?" Her voice was a low murmur. Just low enough that her words would be a strain even for the other wolves to hear, with all the other commotion at the ball. "I thought you didn't want me."

Was there ever a moment that I didn't want her?

"I've wanted you since the first moment I saw you. You're stunning. I'm surprised that none of the other wolves are fighting themselves to the death for a chance to have you."

Jenny hid her blush behind her glass, taking a sip of champagne.

She placed her glass back down on the table, looking me right in the eyes. "Then why don't you want to claim me?"

I'd never noticed the exact color of her eyes before. But now, illuminated by candles, by light glinting off glassware and chandeliers, by the magic of the night, I looked deeply into her eyes: a warm hazel with flecks of green and gold.

"It was never about you." I swallowed, forcing myself to admit it. To get the damning words out. "I was worried about my control."

Jenny had wolf siblings, she would know exactly what that meant. It was a constant struggle to tame the beast. To hold back his wild impulses. Perhaps that was part of the reason why the alpha insisted on balls and formal dinners—to prove that we were more than killing machines.

Shifters with poor control would have a harder time holding back from the wolf's two primal urges—violence. And in the case of mates, fucking.

Jenny swirled her champagne, contemplating the amber whirls of the liquid within. When she looked back at me, it was with a smirk on her lovely face. "Who says that you have to control yourself around me?"

After years convinced that my heart was nothing but a dried out forgotten husk, she proved me wrong. Every one of my senses was ensnared. Utterly captivated by the perfect form of this human girl. With her every move my heart pounded, desire racing through every beat.

Under the full light of the moon's fourth phase, I walked among the shadows of the castle. Taking care to be quiet, as I tracked down my prey.

It hadn't taken long to follow his scent. Humans were predictable. They followed the same patterns. The man's scent remained strongest in the same paths. Ones he'd walked through, and returned to, day after day. It wasn't difficult at all to trail him.

Starting at the soldiers barracks, and following his haunts. The air was thick with his musty body odor. It wouldn't take long before I'd bump into him again.

But when I caught up to him, he wasn't alone.

"Quiet." He hissed, in a strained voice.

Then came the sound of muffled yelps.

It came from within a supply closet, near the guard's barracks.

I unlocked the door with my claws, so silently that it took the soldier a minute to notice. But then again, he was busy. Still in his formal uniform, ironed and pressed for the ball, he was bent over a maid, who seemed far too young. If she was of age, it was just barely. She was blonde, rosy cheeked, and clearly terrified. His hand was jammed up her skirt, rhythmically feeling between her thighs, as his other hand palmed roughly at her breasts.

I didn't even need my wolf senses, to pick up the fear from the girl. She was petrified. With tears pooling at the corner of her eyes.

He didn't even stop, didn't notice anything had changed until I pulled the storage door completely open.

The soldier remained frozen for a moment, hands still in incriminating positions. Then he released her so quickly, she almost dropped to the ground.

"It's not what it looks like." The soldier said in a whiny, almost high pitched voice. Completely different from the voice he'd used when he'd been holding down a defenseless girl. This one, and how many others?

I hadn't gone out looking for an excuse. But if I had walked in on this soldier now. Right now. With no other reason... attacking this girl alone would have been enough.

"I can explain. Sir, if things were over with Jenny, I just had to consider my options..." He seemed to recognize the shit that he was in. His excuses came on fast. They were only half-sensical.

I doubted that this filth had even remained constant to my mate. She said that she'd spent a year pining over him? Yet the same night that a wolf had shown that he was inter-ested, this soldier had gone and put his hands on another woman? One who was clouding the air with the scent of her panic.

I ignored the rest of the sniveling excuses of the man—they didn't mean anything, and weren't worth the effort of shifting through, to sort the meager grains of truth from the lies.

Turning to the girl instead, I gave her the order. "Get out."

If I had a stronger handle on my wolf, I could afford to be more sympathetic. More understanding.

I would have given her advice. Told her to talk to the captain of the guard. Written a formal complaint to the alpha.

But I needed her gone, before the wolf gave in to his rage. I couldn't afford any innocents nearby. Not when they could get hurt in the fallout.

The moment his hands were off her, and she was given the leave to go, the girl bolted out of the supply closet.

Leaving me alone with him.

The soldier opened his mouth again. To beg? To make more excuses? I didn't want to hear any of it.

Claws extended, I struck him. Once. Feeling the squishy give as I pierced through those eyes that had just ogled that poor girl. Feeling the dull resistance as my claws pierced past the gooey fluid of eyes, deep into the skull. Pressing deep enough to hear the crack, as every connection required for living was snapped within the man.

My claws retracted with a wet squelch, as what was left of the soldier crumpled to the floor. I shook off the messy mixture of blood, vitreous and brain fluid. Looks like I would spend more time cleaning up after him than enjoying any revenge.

CHAPTER 9
JENNY

The quiet of the morning was shattered unreasonably early, with a pounding on my door. I jerked out of my perfectly lovely dream. As the banging continued, I muttered obscenities as I pulled off my covers, giving up my hard-earned warmth from my blankets.

"What?" I blurted out as soon as I opened the door, without even checking to see who was here to see me.

Nels was at the door, an uncharacteristic solemn expression on his face. "We need to talk."

I sighed, opening the door wide enough for him. Briefly, I searched for my comfy sweater—the cashmere one. When I didn't find it soon enough, I sat back on my bed, pulling covers around myself like a hibernating bear in a blanket cave.

"This better be good." I muttered in a low voice that Nels would be able to hear nonetheless.

"What were you doing, dancing with Rasmussen last night?"

Oh. That.

Was it really that big of a deal? Such a big deal that I had to be woken up at this ungodly hour? The sun hadn't even finished properly rising yet.

"Why does it matter that I was dancing with him? It doesn't mean anything." I pulled the blankets around myself more firmly. It was not the same as sleeping.

"I've asked around," Nels scowled. "Rasmussen hasn't danced with anyone in at least sixty years."

"So? That means that the man doesn't like dancing. It's not that big of a deal." There was no reason why this conversation had to be had this early. Nels could have just talked to me about it during breakfast. Like a sane person.

"You aren't getting it. The man hasn't been in any relationship. Hasn't been seen with any woman, shifter or otherwise in all that time."

Oh.

Well, I hadn't known he was *still* waiting for his mate. The mate that ended up being me. Human.

"I thought you said you weren't interested in him? That you just wanted to know his name?"

"Maybe I'm not serious about him." I said, refusing to think about how perfectly he'd fit against me as we danced last night. How he'd watched me with smoldering dark eyes.

"Jenny! This is serious! He's not the kind of wolf you can just mess around with. He's extremely dominant. He has a reputation on the battlefield. You should have heard the warnings I was told about him after I shifted."

"What were people saying about him?" My stomach clenched with anxiety.

"Nevermind that. But I still don't get what you are doing messing around with wolves. You do *not* want to get too close to a wolf who hasn't sparked yet—his future mate could come after you. Things can get ugly. Fast."

"Okay, I'm going to show you something, but you have to promise that you aren't going to freak out." Reluctantly, I let the blanket fall off my shoulders. Resigned to the cold air of the morning.

"I swear to the goddess, if you are about to show me a pregnant belly, I'm going to—"

"What?! No! Why would you even think that?" I stripped off the cotton gloves I'd gone to sleep in the night before. I had taken to wearing them more often, now that they mattered. It was a good thing that I had always worn them before, having liked the way they elevated the style of my outfits.

Once the gloves were off, my soulmark was clearly exposed. My mark had healed, though it was still sensitive. Black swirls that swept from the back of my hand, up my wrist and extended up part of my arm. Lines that curled and flowed like ripples, before cutting off sharply. Like something incomplete. Flawed.

"There's no way." Nels brushed against the marks on my palm, as if I was playing some twisted joke on him. As if I'd just drawn on myself with ink that could be rubbed off. Obviously no matter how hard Nels poked at my soulmark, it wasn't going to go away. "Oh, Jenny. How did this happen?"

"I just bumped into him in the woods. The bond sparked between us when he helped me up."

Nels stared at the mark, hard. His face strained, as if he was holding back from rolling his eyes at me, or saying something that I wasn't going to want to hear. After a moment, Nels shook his head. "He isn't going to let you go.

A wolf waiting that long has been waiting for his soulmate."

I shrugged with one shoulder. "He hasn't done anything but wait. Said he needed to think about whether he wanted to be with me or not."

Nels groaned, covering his face in his hands. "All wolves get jealous. It's a part of our nature to be possessive of our mates. Why did you go to the dance with Jayden? You can't just mess around anymore. Not with a mate."

"Well Asher's not possessive. If he cared about me at all, why didn't he invite me to go to the dance?"

"I saw the way he was looking at you at the ball. Everyone saw the way that he was looking at you. Trust me, he's interested."

"What does it matter that he's interested? It's been a week and he hasn't claimed me. So he danced with me last night? He and every other wolf in the castle sees me as nothing more than some lowly human. One dance changes nothing." I was being stubborn and I knew it. But Nels was practically backing me into a corner with this. It's not like I was cheating on the man, or anything like that. He said to my face that he wasn't sure if he wanted to be with me or not.

"You aren't taking this seriously. Did you hear about Jayden? I heard he's gone missing. He had a patrol shift, and just never showed up."

"There was a ball last night. With lots of alcohol. He's probably sleeping off a hangover somewhere." But even as I said the words, that didn't seem right. Abandoning one's post was grounds for termination. Jayden wasn't the irresponsible type.

Though on second thought, that was probably for the better. He'd probably run off scared of what my mate was going to do to him, after he'd gone and shoved his slimy tongue halfway down my throat.

Nils grabbed my shoulders, looking deep into my eyes. "Jenny, I know that you don't want to listen right now. But the soulmark? That changes everything. This is dangerous. Promise me that you'll be careful."

"Fine. I will."

All these men who couldn't figure out what they wanted, it was all a distraction from what really mattered. That wasn't dances, or heated looks or sort-of-soulmates.

I had one week left to become a wolf.

I DID SO MANY CRUNCHES, I wouldn't be surprised if my stomach fell out, dropping away to escape from the rest of my body.

There wasn't any proof that physical training had any impact on one's chances of becoming a shifter. But then again, why did all training programs include physical fitness? It stood to reason that there had to be some sort of a link between them.

I wasn't taking any chances. Every single day for the rest of the week, I trained my body. Hard.

Every morning, even though it was cold out, and miserable, I freed myself from the confines of my blankets, dressed in my sturdiest outdoor apparel and ran. Jogging. The full length of the castle. On the first day, I ran laps until I half-collapsed to the ground with the need to hurl. By the third day, I was running harder, having outrun any nausea. Having pushed past my weak human limits.

Every evening, I committed myself to the texts. Lupine history. The genealogy charts. Astrology. Every wolf text that I could get my hands on. I read, not to learn things—I'd passed all my courses long ago, but to commit as much as I could to memory. If I was going to get in touch with the wolf, I had to mentally connect with her. What better way than to learn as much as possible? As deeply as possible?

I stayed away from everyone. From my siblings, from my former peers and teachers who had looked down on me in disappointment. From everyone who didn't believe in me. All of them. I knew that I had a wolf in me. With time alone, and enough dedication, I was sure that I would bring her out.

This was the moment I'd wished for. Yearned for my entire life. What I'd wished for at the wishing well. It all came down to this.

The full moon hung boldly in the sky. I stepped out from the shadows of the forest, letting the light of the moon trail across my skin. I held myself perfectly still, practically holding my breath. Feeling tingles race up my spine. Bracing for the moment that the wolf would burst free, that my bones would twist and my body would rip apart, releasing my wolf.

I was ready for it. This was the moment that I'd trained for. That I lived and breathed for. I could always feel her, that wild part of me, prowling beneath my skin. I knew that she was there. Goddess, I couldn't wait to meet her.

This was it.

I stood under the moon's light.

Fully human. Fully alone.

I did not become a wolf.

ASHER

My mate had given me no more than a two week deadline. After dancing with her at the ball, I made my decision. I wanted her. I'd always known that I wanted her. Thought that I could be responsible enough to do what was best for her. Safest for her.

It had only taken the smallest hint of what it would feel like to have her taken from me, to break my resolve. Seeing her in the arms of another man was enough to boil my blood. Snap the fragile veneer of control I wrapped around myself, convincing myself that I was something other than a feral beast. The suit, the fine apparel? It was all smoke and mirrors. A mirage, trying to trick me into believing I didn't want to press Jenny to the floor and fuck her in front of anyone who thought they had a chance with her.

It didn't hurt seeing her in that red silk dress. The only thing better would be seeing that dress off of her.

I had to have her.

Yet once I had made up my mind, my mate all but disappeared.

She stopped showing up to the formal dinners, and I

couldn't catch her scent anywhere in the common areas around the castle.

I stalked the infirmary, half out of my mind that something must have happened to her. But she wasn't there. My mate was fine. She was just keeping to herself.

I could scent traces of her on the grounds, but the morning dew tampered just enough with it that I couldn't tell the exact time that she'd been out.

Perhaps she needed time to think things over. Could be that she heard the rumors that her soldier went missing, and that she'd realized that I had something to do with his disappearance.

It was understandable for her to be a little upset that I killed her boyfriend.

I FOUND myself at the front of a familiar portcullis. The General's scent led to his door. I heard the soft padded footsteps within, of the General drawing near, the deep snuffling as he smelled the air, trying to figure out who I was. Then an annoyed snort.

I'd really managed to piss him off with my last visit.

"Before you tell me to get the hell away from your door, I'll admit it. I was wrong." I said, loud enough for his wolf to hear.

I paused, straining to hear any advice through the thick wood. It became clear after a strained minute that no answer was forthcoming.

"I just need some advice. I want to accept my bond with

my human mate. But can you just tell me what I need to do to stop my wolf from hurting her?"

My whole body was tense with anticipation. What did he want me to do? Beg? Go off into the forest and take down an elk, and haul it to his door as a peace offering?

That last thought wasn't a half bad idea. Who didn't like fresh food? Delivered straight to his door, still juicy and dripping. With the heart just stopped mere minutes before? I was half tempted to leave the doorway and try my luck with a bribe, when the General jammed the door open.

"I'd ignore you. It's what you deserve. But it wouldn't be fair for your mate to suffer for your stupidity."

That was fair. I nodded conceding his point.

It was my duty as a mate to do everything in my power to shield Jenny from harm. Especially harm caused by me— which more often than not ended up being the main source of it.

The General opened the door to his rooms. This time around, nothing so blatantly aggressive as blood stained weapons on display. Nothing but some soup, with a plate of bread, next to unlabeled vials. They looked innocent enough, except for the bitter undertones, hanging in the air, smelling faintly like almonds. Cyanide.

So he was testing poisons in his spare time. Like everything else he did, it was tied to the war effort. I wasn't about to ask him what he was doing with it. Not when he seemed annoyed enough talking to me at all in the first place. It could be that he was attempting to hide the scent of poison in food, building up a tolerance for poison as a wolf shifter or something more sinister.

"Kids these days," the General scoffed. "Never been with a human."

I kept the scowl off of my face, though annoyance

itched from beneath my skin threatening to burst through my fingertips. "How does it work? Between a wolf shifter and a human?"

"Are you asking for a female anatomy lesson? Shall I draw you a map?"

"No." My face was so hot, I could feel my ears burning red. "I just want to know how to get close enough to my mate without my wolf trying to rip out her throat."

"Why would you think your wolf is going to kill your mate?" The General leaned against the counter, with a deceptively relaxed expression.

"He's tried to kill women before. Gotten close." I admitted.

"The goddess chose right then. This will force you to practice control."

"Are you suggesting that I use her for practice?" I wouldn't. I'd rather live alone for the rest of my miserable life than put Jenny at risk.

"No matter how wild the wolf, I doubt that he'll be aggressive to a sexual partner. But if he is, you can always redirect it." The General inspected the ends of his nails, brushing against the hard edges and further as if he was imagining the wolf claws bursting through.

"What does that mean?"

"Destroy something else. Tear the sheets. Break the headboard. Rip off clothing. Human women love that shit."

Could that work? It didn't sound entirely too different from what I had to do already when my wolf wanted to kill. Could it really be that simple?

If it was clear that I'd hurt her, I'd let her go. Let her live her life, and choose someone else. I wouldn't interfere. Force myself not to.

But if the General was right? If I could find a way to be with her?

I couldn't stay away without knowing for sure.

Imagining for years what would have happened. What I could have had.

My need for her would drive me insane.

IT WAS EXACTLY two weeks after I'd first sparked with Jenny.

She'd only given me exactly that two weeks.

It hadn't taken half that long for me to make up my mind about her.

But here I was, the deadline had almost passed, and I had no idea where she was.

Fuck social conventions. Fuck it all. I was going to charge into her room, break down her door and tell her in no uncertain terms that she was mine.

I would do it now, if I could fucking find her.

Jenny wasn't in her rooms, or any of the common areas. As far as I could tell, she wasn't in the castle. All of the scent trails I'd found were a week old, and I'd been searching for hours.

It was past dark on the last day of her ultimatum. I would have said something to her before, if I hadn't been worried that she needed space.

It wasn't until I'd ventured down near the stables, that I caught a trace of her scent. She'd passed through, quickly. It seemed like she slipped out of the castle. I followed her trail. Headed deep into the forest, into the heart of a clearing, surrounded by old-growth trees.

Finally I saw her, but something was wrong. Illuminated by the moonlight, she had never looked more beautiful... or more broken. She was half lying on the grass, dirt soiling her fine satin dress. Hunched over with her face pressed into her hands. Sobbing.

"Who hurt you?" I'd failed to keep the rage out of my voice, given by the way Jenny jerked in surprise.

"What are you doing here?" She hastily swiped the back of her palm across the tear streaks on her face, as if that would be enough to erase the evidence. As if the scent of her pain wasn't already hanging in the air, written into every inch of her pores. Daring me to deny it.

Was I too late, once again? How had I failed to protect her?

What the fuck happened?

I grabbed her wrist, turning her delicate limbs over gently. Searching for the cause of this. What the hell had done this? I couldn't find a single cut or mark on her. Not a whiff of another scent on top of hers. Nothing but her rich scent of roses and pine. Intoxicating, but leaving no hint of what had gone wrong.

"Jenny," I cradled her face in my palm, gently pushing her chin up so that she would look me in the eyes. "Tell me what happened to you."

"Nothing. That's what's wrong. Nothing happened."

What?

Did she mean... what?

I know I don't have all that much experience with women, but trying to make sense of that might break my brain.

My nostrils flared, as I tried once more to find the source of her pain. But there wasn't anything. Not a hint of injury, not even bruising. All I could scent was grief pooling off her form in waves.

"I didn't shift." Her eyes clenched shut, and more tears welled up. "This was my last full moon before twenty-two. I am never going to shift. I'm never going to be a normal mate. So just go."

Was the two week deadline never about me at all? Jenny had been counting down to the full moon. Giving herself one last chance to become a wolf.

Did she really think I came here to reject her?

"I don't give a fuck if you're not a wolf." I brushed lightly against the curve of her hips. "I want you just like this."

Her breath shuddered in a shaky inhale. "What are you doing?"

"Giving you my answer." It was what I should have said to her the moment that we first touched. The moment that the soulbond burst into being across our skin. "You're my soulmate. Mine. I accept our bond."

"But, I'm not a wolf." Her eyes were bright, the flecks of green sharper against the teary redness. "You've already lived for longer than I will ever be able to. Is that what you want? To watch me grow old, and then die?"

My gaze was locked on the plump red of her lips as she spoke.

"However long I can have you, I want it all."

Her eyes dropped down, her gaze lowering to my mouth. Slowly. Infinitesimally slowly, she drew closer to me. Leaning in.

Around us, the scent of sorrow in the air faded, replaced by something headier.

The spicy scent of desire.

My lips crashed into hers. Finally, claiming the sweetness of my mate.

I'd waited so long... for her.

She was worth it. I'd wait for her for three lifetimes. A dozen. I'd give them all. Every long year of my life was worth it. Just for this moment with her.

CHAPTER 11

JENNY

Asher broke away from my lips for long enough to whisper into the shell of my ear.

"Tell me to stop." His voice was ragged. Pained.

But nothing had ever felt better than his hard body, pressing desperately against mine.

The darkness in his eyes burned straight into the depths of me. Looking at me and *seeing me*. When everyone else had only ever seen the pieces of me that were lacking.

When I was so used to the disappointment that all of them tried to hide, what was better than this raw feral need?

"Don't stop."

His breathing hitched, and the darkness within his pupils bloomed, before he moved.

He pressed me down, against the grass on the forest floor, and his big body covered mine, straddling me.

The night sky was chilly, but Asher was so warm.

In a move faster than I could see, Asher's claws burst through his fingers.

Before I could protest about things like fittings, and how this was my third favorite dress... Asher sliced through the front of the bodice, tearing until I was fully exposed to him.

I was still half ready to ask him to wait, to see if I could save what was left of my apparel. But then his lips sealed around my nipple, and he sucked. Hard.

I threw my head back, moaning. Digging my nails into the muscles in his back.

Screw the dress.

Asher's hands. His mouth on me. Felt so impossibly good. Running across my body, in feather light touches that were driving me crazy. Every path across my skin burned with the echoes of his caresses.

He caught my palm in his, intertwining our fingers. Connecting our soulmarks. Electricity flickered between our marks, from the center and traveling outwards in a flash of light. I paused, transfixed by the magic of it, watching the blessing of the moon goddess blooming in light across my mark. Connecting us. Looking over to Asher, I caught him staring hard at our marks reacting to one another.

I don't know who moved first, just that the next moment our lips were moving together.

He tasted like desire, raw and unfiltered.

With a wild edge, like he was barely holding on to control.

His fingers bit in too tight sometimes, as he positioned me where he wanted me, pulling off the rest of my clothing. Reducing my dress to shreds.

The feeling of his skin against mine, sparked a fire within me. Igniting me. Awakening a need that burned across everything in my way. His rough hands slid down my thighs, in a heated path straight to my core.

Biting my lip, I held back a whimper as he stroked my clit in a circular pattern. Already so wet, I was practically dripping for him. My pussy was throbbing, high strung. Wound up too tight with nothing to release the tension.

"I need you inside me." My voice felt breathless.

But it was enough. I saw the dip and bob of his Adam's apple as he swallowed.

Then warm prodding as he nudged at my entrance, notching just inside me. And then blissful pressure as he thrust.

Taking me deep.

I moaned—goddess, I don't think I ever moaned that loud in my entire life. Lost in the pleasure. In the stretch. In the heat of him. Canting my hips to take him deeper, wanting him closer. I held him—though Asher was so broad chested that I couldn't wrap my arms completely around him.

Then Asher began to move, thrusting into me hard. He clutched my hip, holding me close. Pressing against me so tightly I could feel the hard ridges of his abs flex as they tensed and bunched against my stomach. I could feel every inch of his cock sliding within me.

Asher pounded into me so hard it was as if I was making love to a force of nature. Something wild. Uncaged. His big body over me and inside of me was everything. Shutting out all of the rest of the world. Grinding against my clit every time he moved. Each thrust creating the most perfect friction. Winding me up higher.

The tension within me coiled. Tightening. Until I was nothing but a taut chord, vibrating with need. I dug my nails into Asher's back, hard enough to draw blood. Arching and pressing myself against him. Needing him closer.

All at once, the tension snapped.

I cried out as I came—harder than ever before in my life. Molten bliss burst from my core, radiating out to every inch of my body in waves. Pleasure washed over me so hard my legs were shaking with it.

All I could do was catch my breath in the aftermath. Panting. Limp and completely boneless.

I think that if I closed my eyes, I'd still be able to see the stars.

"You're so fucking perfect," Asher murmured.

He pressed hot kisses up my neck.

"Beautiful," he whispered in the shell of my ear.

He was circling his hips within me, pressing in deep.

"Strong." His grip on me tightened, like he was having trouble holding back. Like he couldn't get enough. "I want to drench you in my scent, so that everyone who comes near you knows that you're mine."

His eyes burned with a heat that I could feel in my blood. A heat that echoed within me, warming every part of me.

"I'm all yours," my voice was a purr. I couldn't keep the satisfaction out of it. "And I want everyone to know it."

As my words sunk in, Asher grasped me tighter. Holding me in a bruising grip as he pounded into me. Slamming his hips into mine frantically. His rhythm becoming jerky as he chased after his own pleasure.

With one sharp thrust, Asher stilled with a gutteral groan. Within me, I felt him throbbing. Pulse after pulse of warmth filling me.

When Asher finished, he slumped over me pressing his head down into my neck.

I wrapped my arms around him, enjoying the heat of his body in the chill of the night air. Enjoying the peace of the moment. The fact that Asher was heavy and would get uncomfortable soon... or thoughts on how to get back into my rooms now that I was naked in the middle of the forest —those were all concerns for later.

I thought that he'd fallen asleep, until Asher began pressing kisses against my neck. Heated. The touch of his lips was soft, but with a fierce edge. Hungry. Within me, his cock was already starting to harden.

"Again?" I raised an eyebrow. Though he wouldn't see it, as he was too busy pressing red hot kisses to every inch of me that he could reach. I slid my arms down his heavily scratched up back. I'd already done a number on him, was he really back for more already?

Asher pinned my wrists above my head, as he gazed at me with fire in his dark eyes. "I'm never going to have enough of you."

CHAPTER 12

ASHER

FIVE YEARS LATER

My wolf was anxious tonight. Prowling within my body, like my bones were a cage. He'd swipe at them, as if trying to find a weak spot to escape. Snarling within my head, not to be ignored. Tonight was the night of the full moon, he was making it clear that it was past time to let him out.

My wolf had settled down since I'd accepted Jenny as my mate. While he first viewed her with a grumpy acceptance, after Jenny got pregnant with the twins, my wolf became absolutely possessive. Snarling in my mind when anyone got too close to her. He'd ripped into a young wolf who had been eyeing her, and gotten too close. Luckily none of it ended in too much bloodshed. Nothing fatal anyway.

I hadn't had to let him out every full moon. But there was something in the air tonight. A sort of tension, that was grating on him. My human self could even sense a trace of it.

I headed over to the nursery to help Jenny put the kids down for bed. It was a more comfortable room than the rest of the castle. Rather than crown gold molding, and fine oil paintings, this room was painted in soft pastel blues with plush white carpets. Baskets filled to the brim with stuffed toys and train sets.

Jenny was sitting between the boys, on the sofa, reading their bedtime story. They looked so cozy, the boys cuddled up against their mother. Eyes wide as she read about the dragon who fell in love with the princess, or something like that.

Joron and Torsten, or Jory and Tory, as everyone called them. Everyone also said that they looked like miniature versions of me. Which was a shame, when their mother was such a breath-taking beauty.

With their dark mop of curls, scraped elbows and dimpled smiles, the boys were a handful.

Jenny looked up from the pages and smiled at me. "Hello, my love."

I smiled a crooked smile back, not quite sure what I had done to deserve her.

"Alright, come here you rascals." I grabbed both of my squirming sons around the waists, before they could make their giggly escapes, and hauled them off to the bathroom to brush their teeth. Pausing to give Jenny a heated kiss.

"Full moon tonight. You going to be okay?" Checking for any signs of hurt in her eye that she tried to pretend wasn't there. I hated having to leave her. Jenny always became more quiet on nights of the full moon. Which was ridiculous. She didn't need to be a wolf to be the fiercest woman around.

"I'll be fine, I got Trisha helping me watch them." She placed her hand on my cheek, brushing along the side of my jaw.

"I'll see you later." As soon as this wolf calmed down and the kids were in bed. I was coming back for her.

THE LIGHT of the full moon was especially bright tonight, in a cloudless sky.

Within me, my wolf was on alert. Even before I stripped out of my clothes to shift, my wolf was scenting something faint in the air. Something that had him panting and wagging his tail like a puppy.

He was no longer clawing the inside of my chest, fighting against me. It was as if the wolf was tracking... though I couldn't tell what it was that he was hunting. Patiently.

There was something out there.

CHAPTER 13

JENNY

Something was different about the night. It was itching beneath my skin. Like ants crawling all the way through my veins. The air felt too tight, like the walls of the castle were pressing in on me. I had to get out.

I checked in with Trisha to keep watch on the boys for me, and then slipped out into the night. The fact that it was a full moon no longer grated at me. Yes, there could be wolves running about in the forest... but none of them would dare mess with the mate of Asher Rasmussen. According to my siblings, I reeked of the 'big bad wolf' and no one would dare to come too close. Even in wolf form.

That was all fine with me. I walked down a familiar trail through the forest on instinct. Not even recognizing it as the wishing trail, until I had traveled the entire length of it, and was staring for the first time in years at the silvery depths of it. Perfectly reflecting the light of the moon, it was as if the pool had absorbed all of its magic. It was as if the blessing of the moon goddess was here in the water, right within reach.

I'd traveled here so many years ago, craving power. To

unleash the wolf that I somehow still believed in, after all of these years. Instead, the moon goddess had granted me with a dominant and devoted mate. A beautiful family.

Everything that I had never thought to ask for.

I loved my boys with everything in me. And Asher was absolutely lovely. For the first time in years, I saw myself reflected in the milky depths of the wishing well, and I could feel something beyond a secret dream, that piece of my heart... breaking.

While contemplating my silvery reflection, I felt it. Something stirring within me. Something clawing at me from the inside. Awakening. Fighting to break free.

Breathing hard, I clutched at my chest as agony burst through me, shivering through all my limbs. As the bones in my fingers broke, one after another, and my thumb cracked as it changed location, moving up my forearm—What was this?

It wasn't until the skin on my face split, and the canine jaw forced its way through my skin that I finally realized what was happening.

But... *how?*

After all this time? No. I was too old. This wasn't possible. This wasn't supposed to be possible.

Yet, whether I believed it or not, this transformation was happening. My bones shifted within my body, as another form awakened.

She had been sleeping. I could feel her during the transformation, stretching. Yawning. Shaking the years off of her fur, even as my skin was stretched out and reformed. Even as her gray pelt erupted across every inch of my body.

I fell to the ground onto four feet—paws.

Shifted.

Into the wolf that no one had believed existed.

My human self was frozen. Paralyzed with disbelief. But my wolf, she knew exactly what to do. She arched her head up to the full bright light of the moon, and let loose a howl. Her high notes burst into the quiet of the night. Long and aching.

But not alone.

Not for long.

My wolf's cry was answered by a return howl—a howl that I somehow already recognized. I knew him. It didn't matter that I had never specifically listened for him on any of the nights he'd slipped out to shift into his other self. The deepest part within me already knew him.

A wolf, black as pitch, was running through the forest. Making his way to me. Even if I hadn't recognized his coloring, I would know exactly who he was. I would recognize him anywhere.

He approached me, shivering with anticipation. Each step, slow and precise, until he stopped a few feet away and came no closer. The dark wolf whined, digging his claws into the ground.

Something was holding him back. It was as if he was at war with himself.

This happened sometimes when the man held back the beast. But why would he do that? Did that mean...

Did Asher not recognize me?

The human part of me rolled my eyes. *Men.*

I couldn't explain anything in this form. Couldn't help my mate understand what was happening.

Though I had only let her out briefly, after waiting all my life to meet her, I had to call back my wolf. Promising her silently that I'd let her out again soon.

As my bones realigned, snapping in places and the fur slipped away from my skin, I couldn't hold myself up. I fell to the ground. Limbs shaking with the strain of holding up my newly formed body. Nothing would have been easier than to fall to the ground and close my eyes. Sleeping off the pain in the dead of the night. But I refused. I breathed deep gulps, trying to force myself to stand.

Shaking, and shivering in the cool night air, a hand reached out for me. Asher, had quietly transformed back and offered to help me to my feet.

A bit my lip, as I forced myself to move my reborn body. My shaky hand reached out to grab his.

The moment that our hands touched, electricity burned across my newborn skin. Bright, silvery light glowed within the center of our marks, spreading outwards in new spirals. In swirls and curves revealing patterns of moon phases. Of all the cycles of the blessing of the goddess.

Our bond was complete.

About the Author

After years of writing, Miyo decided to unleash her wolfish fantasies upon the world.

Shifters. Dominant Alphas. Sweet love and dark fantasy. Miyo is writing this for every reader who wants their characters bent over chairs and called a good girl. For everyone who wants to forget their day-jobs and responsibilities and curl up to read something spicy. For everyone who wants to unlock a world that's just a little bit wild.

instagram.com/miyohunter
tiktok.com/@miyohunter

Moonlight Mates

Moonlight Reborn

He was the most dominant wolf in the pack and I'm the bullied outcast he hates until his skin touched mine, electricity sparked. Marking us. We both knew what it meant—a soulbond.

Moonlight Shifter

Finding your soulmate is every wolf shifter's dream—except mine. I'm already in love. So when destiny revealed my mate, I did the only thing I could. I ran from him. But no matter how strong I am, a lone wolf is vulnerable. When I'm captured, the only one who can come for me, is the mate I'd rejected.

Moonlight Claimed—coming soon!

We hid our identities at the Shifter's Masked Ball, but I still managed to find my soulmate among the sea of masked faces and smothered scents. While I thought he was everything I'd ever wanted, I realized several sweaty and delicious minutes later that I'd made a horrible mistake. Is it too late to reject him now that my fate is sealed? Or could this unlikely bond be exactly what I've been waiting for?

Omegaverse

His Gold Pack Omega

A shattered omega socialite, rejected by society.

After what I went through, becoming an outcast was the only

way to survive. But now none of the laws protecting omegas apply to me. I hired him to be my bodyguard. He's all raw strength, gorgeous and protective.I feel drawn to him, and the heat in his gaze makes me feel alive again. For the first time in years, I feel safe. But how can I let him in without letting him see the broken thing I've become?

*Knot Your Basic B*tch*

Who wants a shot at love and a pack of their very own? Not this b*tch. Nothing will stand between me and my dream—to finally get a nice calm secretarial job—not even sexy twins or chiseled abs. At least, that's what I tell myself. But when destiny crashes into all my careful plans with HOT scent matches, will I be able to cling to my hope for a simple life? Or will I let them sweep me off my feet?